World of Reading

Disney

FROZEN

An Icy Monster

Written by

Megan Ilnitzki

Illustrated by the

Disney Storybook Art Team

Disney Press

Los Angeles • New York

Printed in China
First Box Set Edition, August 2016
1 3 5 7 9 10 8 6 4 2
FAC-025393-16127
ISBN 978-1-4847-7382-6

It is a sunny day.
Anna and Elsa want
to play outside.

The sisters decide to
have a bike race.

Anna takes the lead.
She is winning.

Elsa uses her magic.
She beats Anna.
“No fair,” Anna says.

Anna sees their friends.
They look upset.

Anna stops her bike.
She wants to know
what is wrong.

Sven and Kristoff saw something
in the mountains.
It was very big.

The sisters agree
to help them find it.

Elsa and Anna
change their clothes.
They find Olaf.
He wants to go, too.

Anna and her friends
go up the mountain.
It is snowing hard.

Elsa and Olaf
like the snow.
They play together.

Elsa and Olaf look
at their friends.
They are covered in snow.

Elsa uses her magic
to clear the snow away.

The friends want
to find the monster.

There is too much snow.
They do not know
where to look.

Olaf hears a noise.
He thinks it is Sven's belly.

Anna knows better.
It is the monster!

The friends follow
the loud noise.
It is too hard to see
through the trees.

Elsa has an idea.
She builds ice stairs.
Now the friends can see
over the trees!

Kristoff, Anna, and Elsa
climb the stairs.
They see the trees shake.

Olaf and Sven
wait on the ground.
They make snowmen.

Anna sees something coming.
She tells Olaf to hide.

Olaf does not hear.
He is watching a bird.

Something comes
through the trees.

It is not a monster.
It is Marshmallow!

Olaf hugs his friend.
Olaf's friend
hugs him back.
It is a very big hug!

The big snowman is happy
to see his friends.
It is lonely
on the mountain.

Kristoff has an idea.
The big snowman can
help him deliver ice.

The big snowman is happy.
Now he will not
be alone!